ZEPPELIN

78

No.9

NYla Bergson

The MODERN STORY BOOK

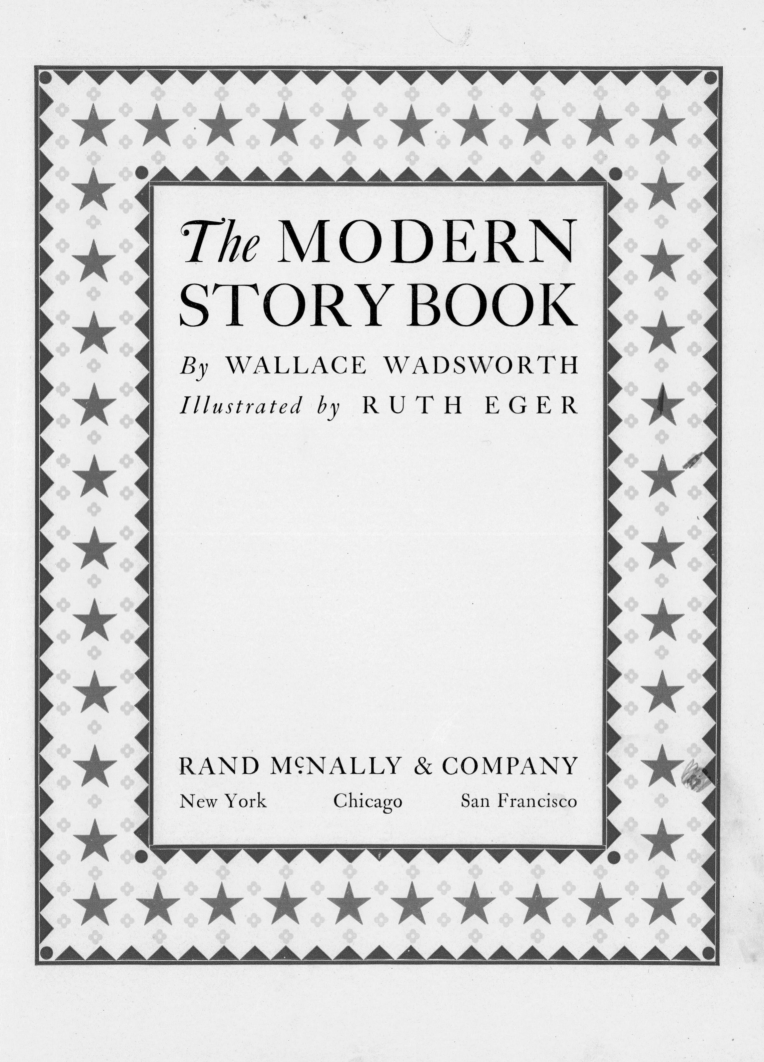

The MODERN STORY BOOK

By WALLACE WADSWORTH

Illustrated by RUTH EGER

RAND McNALLY & COMPANY

New York   Chicago   San Francisco

Printed in the United States of America

20MA-31

The Contents

Illustrations in Color

Illustrations in Color *(continued)*

The MODERN STORY BOOK

BUT STILL OLD JEFF OILED AND TOOK CARE OF NUMBER NINE

The Fire Engine That Grew Too Old

NUMBER Nine was a Fire Engine—not a very big one, however, for he was one of the first automobile Fire Engines ever made. Since he had been built, many larger engines had come to the city, and these had crowded him out of one great engine house after another. At last, he had been forced to make his home in a little engine house out on the edge of the city. Here there were not many fires and so he had little work to do.

When Number Nine had been a new engine, with red paint shining as bright as a looking-glass, Old Jeff had become his driver. Old Jeff was proud of Number Nine, and soon Number Nine grew to be proud of him. For the new driver was one of the best firemen in all the city and had many medals to pin on his chest because of his brave deeds.

Now when Number Nine was crowded out of the big stations by the newer Fire Engines and sent, at last, to the little engine house away out on the very edge of town, Old Jeff was sent along with him. For as Number Nine grew old, Old Jeff grew older. And people thought that neither of them could be of much use at a big fire now.

Number Nine did not like to sit in the engine house day after day without any work. Old Jeff did not like it, either. But the Fire Chief never sent them to a big fire any more. All they could find to do was, once in a great while, to put out some easy little fire.

Old Jeff used to talk to Number Nine when he was polishing his bright red paint and brass work.

"They think we are too old to be of any use," he would grumble to Number Nine. "Yet we know more about putting out big fires than any other fireman or engine in the city. They have

sent us out here, almost in the country, where there is nothing to do. First thing you know, they will want to throw us both on the scrap pile."

"Our chance will come," Number Nine would reply to Old Jeff. "Some day these new firemen and engines will get to a fire too big for them. Then they will have to call on us to help them out. So keep up your courage, Old Jeff. Oil my bearings and tighten my bolts, and we shall be ready to show them when our chance comes."

Every time the fire alarm rang in the little engine house, Number Nine would tremble a little, he was so eager to go. And Old Jeff would stand ready to jump into the driver's seat. But months went by, and though many fire alarms were rung, never did they hear the signal calling them to help put out a fire.

Winter came on, and still the signal did not ring for Number Nine. And then, one morning, the coldest day of the year, a very big fire broke out downtown. A tall building was on fire, and before long the blaze had caught in several other offices near by.

As the signals rang in the little engine house, calling for one Fire Engine after the other, Number Nine and Old Jeff trembled with eagerness. Old Jeff walked about Number Nine, squirting oil and making sure that everything was spick and span. And all the time he talked to Number Nine.

"Will they call us this time, Number Nine? This is a big fire, but they think we are too old to be of any use at a big fire. Perhaps they will forget all about us again."

But this time Number Nine felt sure — clear down in the middle of his machinery — that he and Old Jeff would be called.

"No, Old Jeff," he said. "They will not pass us by. This fire is too big for all those young firemen and new engines to handle by themselves. They will have to call out us old-timers, who know more about fighting big fires."

And Number Nine was right; for just then the signal rang that they had long been waiting for.

Whee-e-e-e! Old Jeff and Number Nine were going to the big fire at last!

Old Jeff sprang into his seat, and Number Nine was ready to go as the broad doors of the little engine house swung open. They dashed out so quickly that the other firemen who rode on Number Nine hardly had time to put on their helmets and rubber coats and swing aboard.

Along the snowy streets they roared, going downtown to the big fire. Number Nine's siren squealed, "Oo-wee-oo-oo-oo! Get out of the way! Out of the way! We're going to the big fire! Oo-WEE-oo-o-o!"

When they got downtown, Old Jeff could see the clouds of smoke from the burning buildings. "We're coming to the big fire," he called. "Do your best, Number Nine!"

Number Nine was going too fast to say anything, but he rolled along at his best speed. Soon they

THEY ROLLED UP VERY NEAR THE BURNING BUILDINGS

passed the fire lines. Policemen were holding the people back in order to give the firemen plenty of room.

They rolled up very near to the burning buildings, and then Old Jeff said, "The worst fire is in the Smith Building, Number Nine. These new firemen don't know how to fight a big fire. They have forgotten all about the alley hydrant behind the building."

Just then the Fire Chief ran

THEN OLD JEFF SAID, "THE WORST FIRE IS IN THE SMITH BUILDING"

JUST THEN THE FIRE CHIEF RAN UP

up. "You here, Old Jeff?" he cried.

"All here, both Old Jeff and Number Nine," Old Jeff called back.

"You can help Number Forty with its pumping," said the Chief. "We need all the water we can throw, and more, too."

"The place for Number Nine is at the alley hydrant, behind the Smith Building," said Old Jeff.

"Too dangerous," said the Chief. "The walls may fall any moment. We need the water back there badly, but I won't tell any man to take up his post there."

"Ho-ho!" laughed Old Jeff. "Number Nine and I will give you all the water you want from the alley. Come along, Number Nine." And Number Nine ran along.

The alley was a fearful sight. Up above, red flames and smoke poured from the Smith Building. Farther along, another building's walls had fallen, and the fire was leaping out in great flames. All around hung ice and icicles from the water the firemen had thrown onto the fire, trying to put it out.

But Old Jeff and Number Nine did not hold back. Up the alley they went to the hydrant, almost to the fallen walls. There Old Jeff stopped Number Nine and quickly fastened his pumping hose. At the same time, firemen stretched hose lines from Number Nine, running them inside the burning building, so that they could fight the fire in a new place.

"All right, boys," called Old Jeff, above the roar of the fire and the roar of Number Nine's strong motor. "Now you'll have water as long as there is any Number Nine or Old Jeff."

And then Number Nine started pumping water onto the big fire just as fast as he could. Whee-e-e! It was hard work, but Number Nine thought it was the greatest fun he had ever known. He trembled with joy as he felt the thousands and thousands of gallons of water rush through his pump and on through his hose lines as fast as he could push them forward.

Sometimes the heat from the flames was so great that it blistered Old Jeff's face and Number Nine's bright red paint. Sometimes, in spite of the hot fire, the strong cold wind from the street blew over them and froze the water about them into glittering ice.

Before very long, Number Nine was covered with ice, and Old Jeff looked like an ice man. But still Old Jeff oiled and took care of Number Nine, and Number Nine pumped away as hard as ever.

OLD JEFF QUICKLY FASTENED THE HOSE

"I'm afraid the wall is going to fall before long," Old Jeff whispered to Number Nine. "It is getting very weak."

Number Nine did not care very much whether the wall fell on him or not, but he hated to have it fall on Old Jeff.

"Fill up my oil cups as full as you can, Old Jeff," he said. "Fix me up so that I can run for a long time. Then, if the wall starts to fall, you crawl under me, and I will keep you from getting hurt."

So, presently, when some bricks crashed down near by, Old Jeff looked up and saw that the wall was just about to fall. He finished filling another oil cup for Number Nine, and then, just in time, he crawled under the brave little Fire Engine. With a mighty crash, a part of the wall toppled and fell upon Number Nine.

"Are you hurt badly, Number Nine?" called Old Jeff.

"Not badly, Old Jeff," called back Number Nine. "The wall is crushing me so heavily that I'm afraid I shall burst my tires, and I am somewhat bent up, but my pump and motor are not hurt. I can run for a long, long time yet. Are you hurt, Old Jeff?"

"Just a broken ankle, where a brick hit me," said Old Jeff. "But perhaps I can crawl around and give you a little oil when you need it. We'll show them yet, won't we, Number Nine?"

After the wall had fallen, the water from the hose lines came over onto Number Nine more than ever. By and by, so much water had fallen on Number Nine and on the heavy wall on top of him that nothing could be seen of the little Fire Engine. Only a great lump of glittering ice filled the alley.

The ice and wall together grew so heavy that Number Nine

ONLY A GREAT LUMP OF GLITTERING ICE FILLED THE ALLEY

burst all his tires. "Bang! Pop-pop! Hiss-s-ss!"— but still he kept right on pumping.

"I need oil, Old Jeff," he would call once in a while.

And Old Jeff, in spite of his broken ankle, would manage to wiggle around under all the ice and pieces of wall that covered them up and give Number Nine a drink of oil in his oil cups. And Number Nine would then go on pumping water onto the big fire, harder than ever.

After a while, the firemen began to put the fire out. At last, when it was no longer a big fire, nor even a medium-sized one, but only a small one, the Fire Chief thought of Old Jeff and Number Nine. As quickly as he could, he ran to the alley where they were. He became very sad when he saw how the wall had fallen.

He called some firemen to help him. "The wall fell on Old Jeff," he said. "Get tools, and we'll dig him out. Poor old fellow, he would risk it here. Now the wall has fallen on him."

So the firemen got tools, and they began to dig. After they had dug a little while, one of the firemen said to the Chief, "What's that sound I hear? It comes from under this pile of ice and bricks."

The Chief listened. "Why, it is old Number Nine, still pumping away!" he cried. "Hurry, boys! Perhaps Old Jeff is all right, also."

So the firemen dug harder than ever, and before long they came upon Old Jeff under the ice and broken wall which Number Nine had held up off him. And Old Jeff was giving Number Nine another drink of oil when they found him.

The Chief felt very proud of Old Jeff and Number Nine, because of the brave way they had kept on working. It was because Number Nine had kept on pumping so strongly that they had put out the big fire as soon as they had. All the citizens of the town were proud, also, and they gave Old Jeff another medal to wear.

As for Number Nine, everybody thought he was a wonderful old Fire Engine. He was given a new coat of bright red paint, and his brass work was shined until it looked like gold. Then he was paraded through the city to the biggest engine house. And there he stands yet, with a little brass plate on his side which tells of the brave work he has done. Old Jeff is there to take care of him, and to tell how Number Nine saved his life and helped put out the big fire.

So they are both quite happy, in spite of the fact that the Chief won't let them go to fires any more. The Chief thinks that now they really are too old.

Of course, Old Jeff and Number Nine know better than that. It is a good joke between them. But since they have had their share in the worst fire that the city has ever had, they are willing to stand aside now and give younger firemen and Fire Engines a chance.

AFTER EACH BITE SHE WOULD SWING AROUND AND DROP THE WHOLE MOUTHFUL

The Hungry Steam Shovel

THE Engineer who ran the big Steam Shovel called her "Hungry Lizzie," because, he said, she was always ready to eat a big hole right down in the ground or to bite into a hill. Hungry Lizzie didn't mind what her Engineer said about her; she liked him, anyway.

She belonged to a big construction company which built new buildings. Lizzie's work was to make great holes in the ground where later large buildings would be put up. All day long Hungry Lizzie would do nothing but take huge bites of earth and stone with her sharp-toothed shovel. After each bite she would swing around and drop the whole mouthful into a heavy motor truck that stood there waiting to carry it away. So big were her bites that one was all a strong truck could carry.

Sometimes Lizzie would work out in the country, eating a great deep ditch, or canal, across marshy land. When the

[23]

water from the marsh ran into the ditch, the fields on each side would become dry enough to be planted with corn and potatoes.

But all her life, no matter what she was doing, Lizzie had always been hungry. She had never enjoyed anything more than chewing up the earth in great mouthfuls. And then, at last, something dreadful happened. Hungry Lizzie lost her appetite!

The big Steam Shovel had been eating a wide, deep hole in the ground, where later on the heavy feet of a tall building would rest, when suddenly she no longer felt hungry. Instead of taking a truckload of earth and rock at one bite, as she had always done before, she just nibbled a little dust.

"Here, here! What's wrong with you, Hungry Lizzie?" cried her Engineer. "What do you mean by taking such a small bite?"

"I'm just not hungry any more," explained Lizzie.

"Why, I never heard of such a thing!" exclaimed her Engineer in surprise.

"Nor I, either," said the Steam Shovel, "but it's true just the same."

"Let's try it again," said the Engineer.

But try as they would, Hungry Lizzie could not swallow a truckload at a bite. All that she could do was to nibble a tiny bit of dirt and rock each time.

"I can't understand what's wrong with her," the Engineer said to the Foreman. "We'll have to get another Steam Shovel to take her place. I'll send her out to the storage yard until I get the time to go over her and put her into good shape again."

So another Steam Shovel

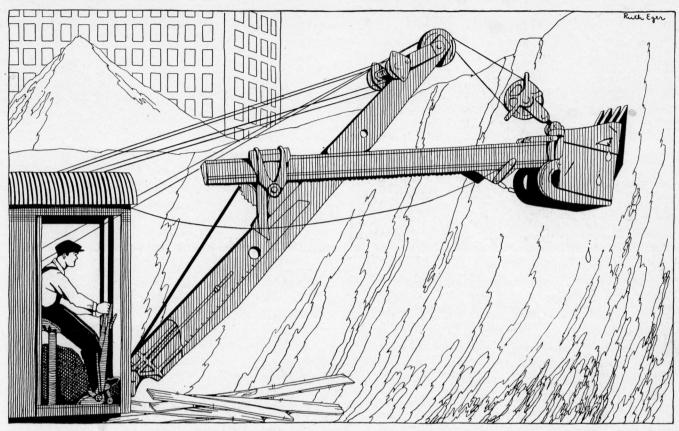

ALL THAT HUNGRY LIZZIE COULD DO WAS TO NIBBLE A TINY BIT

took poor Lizzie's place, and she was driven away to the big yards of the construction company, out near the edge of the city.

Three boys lived near the big storage yards—Johnny and Jerry and Pete. They often played about among the heavy graders and scrapers and other things stored there. When they saw Lizzie taking her place among the other machines, they hurried over to climb on her and see just what she was like. The boys had played in the yard so often that they knew all the machines and used to talk to them.

"Did you get tired of working?" Jerry asked Lizzie. "Is that why they sent you here to rest up?"

"Oh, no," said Lizzie. "I was not tired of working. I just lost my appetite all at once, and then

I couldn't eat big bites of earth and rocks any more."

"Perhaps you should take a pill," Johnny, the littlest boy, told her. "That's what I have to do sometimes, when I don't feel like eating."

"Tut-tut!" answered Lizzie. "Who ever heard of a Steam Shovel taking a pill?"

"PERHAPS YOU SHOULD TAKE A PILL," JOHNNY TOLD HER

The oldest boy laughed; he had thought of a new game.

"I'll bet we could make a pill for you that would give you an appetite again," he said to Lizzie.

"Of course we can," cried Johnny and Jerry. "Let's make it now."

So Johnny and Jerry and Pete ran off to make a pill for the big Steam Shovel, while Hungry Lizzie sat back and laughed heartily at such a queer idea.

"Here's some tar in this old tar barrel," cried Johnny. "We'll use a lot of it."

The boys took all the tar that they could get, and when the hot sun had softened it, they made a great big black tar ball, almost as big as their heads.

Then they hunted about until they found other things to mix with the tar. They found some sulphur, and they found some axle grease and some rosin, and some sticky old paint in cans that had been thrown away. All of this they put together into a great round lump as big as a basket ball. This was the pill they were going to give to the big Steam Shovel to make her hungry again.

"My goodness!" cried Lizzie, when she saw what the boys were bringing her. "What's that dreadful-looking thing you have?"

"It's your pill," said the boys. "After you take it, you'll be hungry again."

"Dear me," said Lizzie, "I'm quite sure that it will do all sorts of things to me. What a big pill it is! And how shall I take it?"

The boys hadn't thought of that. One was sure that the best way to give a pill to a Steam Shovel was to drop it down the smokestack. Another said that it should be put in the sharp-toothed shovel itself. But the best suggestion of all, they thought, was that they build a hot fire in the big Steam Shovel's fire box and then throw the pill into the center of the fire.

So Johnny and Jerry and Pete kindled a fire in the fire box and shoveled in coal until the fire was burning very hotly, indeed.

"Gracious!" Lizzie said to herself, "it's a good thing that my boiler is still full of water; otherwise, this hot fire would go badly with me."

Since she had plenty of water in her boiler, the fire did her no harm. But it did begin to make so much steam inside her that Lizzie almost wanted to start working again and chew up the earth in great mouthfuls.

"Now!" cried Pete, when the fire was burning steadily. "Give her the pill!"

And while Johnny held the door of the fire box open, Jerry threw in the big pill of tar and grease and rosin and paint. Johnny slammed the fire door shut in a hurry. Then the boys hopped out on the ground and stood to one side to see how the big Steam Shovel would act when she tasted the medicine they had made for her.

All at once, as they watched, a thick, heavy smoke began to pour from Lizzie's smokestack. The sound of her draft became a roar as the fire suddenly grew many times hotter from all the fast-burning things which were in the pill. The fire grew so very hot that Lizzie's boiler made more steam than it could hold. Her safety valve popped open with a great hissing sound to let the extra steam escape.

As her smoke grew thicker and her fire grew hotter, all the

soot and ashes in Lizzie's flues were blown out through her stack. Now her fire could breathe better, and suddenly, almost before she knew it, Lizzie felt herself getting hungry again. All at once she wanted to bite deeply into the ground and eat out great mouthfuls of earth and stone, just as she had done so many times before.

"How do you feel now?" the boys called to her.

"Fine!" she cried. "I'm hungry again! Jump up on me and pull all my levers and turn all my do-jiggers, so that I can move along and get something to eat."

The boys were very proud to think that their medicine had done the big Steam Shovel good. They jumped aboard her and began pulling all her levers and turning all her do-jiggers at once, just as she had told them to do.

And then suddenly Hungry

ALL THE SOOT AND ASHES IN LIZZIE'S FLUES WERE BLOWN OUT

Lizzie began to move forward on her broad caterpillar feet, and her heavy shovel began dipping up and down. Her whistle tooted, her big sharp-toothed shovel swung down to the ground and grabbed up a huge bite of earth. Twisting about, Lizzie threw this bite to one side and then, quick as a flash, she took another bite right beside the first.

"Yum-yum!" she mumbled, as she kept on eating as fast as she could.

When the boys saw her making a big hole right in the center of the construction yard, they became a little frightened. But they were having fun watching Hungry Lizzie and were not quite ready to run away and leave her all alone, yet.

"Shovel more coal on my fire, boys," Lizzie called to them. "More coal! More coal!" and she

"YUM-YUM!" SHE MUMBLED

kept right on snapping at the ground.

Perhaps it was the pill she had taken, or her hot fire, or perhaps it was the way that the boys had

THE BOYS HURRIED HOME FAST.

pulled her levers and twisted her do-jiggers all at the same time, that made Lizzie eat into the ground so very much faster than usual. But, anyhow, it was only a very short time until she had dug herself into a hole that was very long and wide and far deeper than she was tall.

She had bitten her way down into the ground so quickly that the boys had hardly noticed what was happening. Suddenly some graders and scrapers near the edge of the big hole began to tumble down the steep sides and crash against Hungry Lizzie with a great clatter.

"Oo-o-oh! Look what's happened!" cried Johnny.

"We've got to stop her!" shouted the other two boys, as they saw how fast Hungry Lizzie was biting her way into the ground. They pulled and twisted all her levers and do-jiggers again and would not let her have any more coal in her fire box. Then they opened her whistle, "Toot-toot! Too-oo-oot!" so that much of her steam could blow away with a great noise. Before long they had made her stop eating, even though she was still as hungry as ever.

Jerry and Johnny and Pete climbed out of the big hole which Hungry Lizzie had made and hurried home as fast as they could go. They had thought it a great joke at first to give a pill to the big Steam Shovel, but now they were rather worried.

"It was a crazy idea, even if it did work," Pete told his two friends. "Who ever heard of a piece of machinery taking pills?"

As for Hungry Lizzie, she grew hungrier than ever as she waited at the bottom of her hole through all the long afternoon. And because she was so very hungry, she grew more and more unhappy. Finally, something happened which made her feel much better.

"What in the world are you doing down there?" an angry voice said from the edge of the big hole she had dug. The Steam Shovel looked up to see her Engineer standing there looking down at her.

"What do you mean by digging a hole in the yard this way?" he shouted at her, waving his arms about.

Hungry Lizzie felt a little ashamed now of what she had done.

"Oh, I just took a pill to cure my loss of appetite," she said. "Then I became so hungry that I couldn't wait to start eating. I began biting into the ground right where I stood, and before I knew it, I had eaten this hole in the earth. But I'm so hungry that I shall never lose my appetite again, and I can bite away harder and faster now than I ever could before."

When the Engineer heard this, he forgot his anger and became so excited that he tumbled over the edge of the hole and rolled down the steep side until he landed, kerthump! hard against Hungry Lizzie. He was all shaken up, but he forgave the big Steam Shovel for that, also. He was so glad that she had found her appetite again.

The next day, as soon as he could get her out of the big hole, the Engineer took Hungry Lizzie back to work again. And from that time on, she worked away better than ever. She was always hungry and ate away the earth and stone faster than she had done before. She never had to take another pill, which was probably just as well. It would have been very hard to find anyone who could have made a pill for her like the one the three boys gave her to cure her appetite.

WHEN HE WAS BUILT, ZEP WAS THE BIGGEST DIRIGIBLE IN THE WORLD

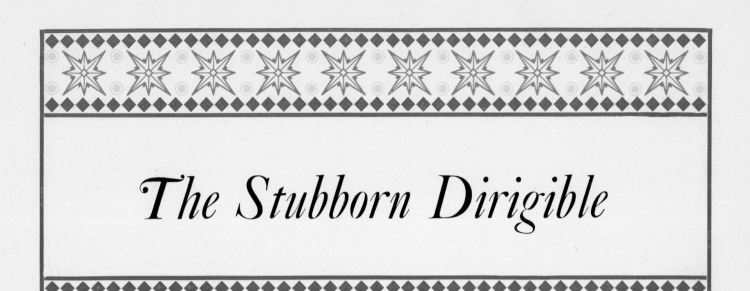

The Stubborn Dirigible

ZEP was restless, and he moved a little from side to side in the big hangar which was his home. "Dear me," he complained, "but I'm tired of staying shut up in here. I wish they would take me out on a nice long flight. I need fresh air."

When he was built, Zep was the biggest Dirigible Airship in the world. He was as long as a city block and so big around that a circus tent could almost have been set up inside him. He lived in an enormous building, called a hangar, large enough to hold him and three or four smaller Dirigibles, too.

Zep was strongly made, with a stout framework of metal called "duralumin," which was light as well as very strong. This was covered tightly with a thick, tough fabric, woven like cloth. It was silvery in color and made Zep look like a giant silver fish when he flew high in the air. Inside, Zep was filled with many round balloons, or "balloonets" as they were called. They held the light gas that lifted Zep into the clouds.

The gas in his "balloonets" was so much lighter than air that, when he was turned loose from the ground, the air would push Zep upward—just as water makes a cork rise to the top.

Underneath, Zep had little cars, called gondolas, which were fastened to him and extended out on each side. Every car held a strong motor that turned a big propeller. When all the motors began to work and all the propellers to turn, Zep would begin to swim through the air as fast as a train could run, or even faster, perhaps. There were big fins fastened on his tail to guide him to this side or that side, and to make him rise higher or sink lower in the air.

It had been a long time, however, since Zep had flown. He was getting tired of staying shut up in the big hangar. So one day, when the Commander who had charge of him decided to go for a long flight through the air, Zep was very glad. The Commander called all the men of his crew and other men, too, to help get Zep out of the hangar into the open air.

First, the big doors at the end of the hangar were opened. Then the Commander and his crew climbed up into the great Dirigible. The men on the ground caught hold of the ropes fastened to Zep and began to slowly walk with him through the big, open doors. There were so many holding the ropes that Zep could not rise from the ground.

Outside the hangar Zep's motors were started, and when the Commander gave the order, the men on the ground let go of the ropes. Ah! Zep was free. The big Dirigible started to rise and then, because his motors were working and his propellers turning, he began to swim away through the air just like a big silver fish.

High up, Zep and his crew sailed along for many miles. The green fields down below looked like little squares on a patchwork quilt, and the rivers seemed to be just silver threads. The towns over which they flew were dark spots with the thin lines of their streets running crisscross through them.

"My, but this is wonderful," said Zep to himself. For he liked to fly, and always grew restless when he was shut up in his hangar. "This is such a wonderful day. If it would only stay like this, I should like to sail on forever. I'm afraid, though, that a storm is coming up—I feel it in the air— my ribs tingle. The Commander had better not take me too far from home, or he may get lost in the storm and not be able to find his way back to the hangar."

But the Commander did not think about any storm, because the weather was so nice and the sun was shining so brightly. Such a thing never occurred to him until all at once black clouds began to pile up along the edge of the sky straight ahead of Zep.

"Looks like a storm coming, Commander," said one of the other officers in the Dirigible.

"Yes," agreed the Commander, "and it looks like a bad one, too. We'll go ahead against it for a little while, and then if it gets too strong for us, we'll turn back home."

So Zep sailed on a little while longer toward the big, black clouds. He was going so fast and the storm was coming so swiftly that it was only a very short time until he was right in the middle of a blanket of clouds. It grew as dark as night, and the wind blew fiercely in every direction.

As big as he was, Zep was tossed up and down by the angry wind. He was shoved to one side and then to the other until he began to groan and creak all over.

"The wind is getting too strong for us," said the Commander finally. "The only wise thing to do is to go back to the hangar."

So he gave orders for Zep to be turned about. The roaring wind twisted and shoved the big Dirigible as he turned, until the men bobbed and bounced around in him like dried peas in a big bottle.

"Oh, my poor ribs!" groaned Zep.

No sooner had Zep turned around and started to fly back toward his hangar than the storm became worse. Zep was blown one way for a while and then an-other way for another while. It was so dark and the rain and the clouds were so thick that the Commander and his men could not see the earth

THE ROARING WIND TWISTED HIM

— "OH, MY POOR RIBS!" GROANED ZEP

far below. They became lost. No one knew just exactly how to get back home again.

"They are guiding me in the wrong direction," sputtered big

Zep to himself, as he fought on through the terrible storm. "They are lost. If they keep on as they're headed now, they will never get back."

The winds blew and the thunder crashed. Zep had a hard time flying on at all. His strained ribs began to hurt him more than ever.

"Oh, my goodness," he growled, after a little while. "I had better think of something to do, or we shall never get back to the hangar."

And so, as he flew along through the black storm, Zep thought to himself, "I'll just have to turn myself around and go right along as I think best, no matter what the Commander wants me to do. He will be very angry if I don't obey him, but if I do obey him, we shall never get home tonight."

The man who was steering the big Dirigible suddenly felt the steering handle twist out of his hands. Zep had turned himself to go another way.

"That wind is terribly strong, sir," the man cried to the Commander. "It twisted the rudders so hard that the handle spun away from me."

"Get back on your course," ordered the Commander, and the man again tried to guide the big Dirigible. He tugged at the steering handle, but it would not move.

"It won't answer the helm!" cried the man.

The Commander, himself, then tried to turn the big Dirigible back again. But Zep was stubborn. He would not allow his course to be changed the least little bit.

"It's jammed!" cried the Commander, angry as Zep knew he would be. "Take a crew of men and examine the steering apparatus closely. If it is damaged so that we can't fix it, we may find ourselves out in the ocean before this storm is over."

"Yes, sir," said the man, and away he went.

He and his helpers looked Zep over, but they could find nothing wrong. They did not know it, but the matter was that Zep wouldn't be turned in any direction except the one he knew was right.

At last the men reported that they could find nothing wrong. The Commander now became more worried than ever.

"As nearly as I can guess," he said, "we are going farther away from home all the time. No tell-

THE CLOUDS WERE SO THICK THAT THE MEN COULD NOT SEE THE EARTH

ing where this storm may carry us, since we cannot steer ourselves."

But they really were not sailing farther away from home, as the Commander feared. Instead, the big Dirigible was going right toward his hangar as fast as he could go. He was so anxious to get back to shelter, out of the fierce storm, that he would not let anything turn him aside. The wind tried to blow him this way and that. But each time Zep would turn right back in the direction of the hangar and fly along as fast as he could, in spite of all the wind could do.

On and on he flew, despite the clouds and the wind. At last he began to turn his nose a little toward the earth.

"We're going down!" cried one of the men, who felt the big Dirigible turning to fly toward the earth.

The Commander tried to force Zep to go higher again, but he could not. Then he became frightened. Surely, he thought, they were going to be dashed to pieces against the ground.

But big Zep was only headed for home. He flew through the clouds, going down a little all the time, and suddenly he came out below a bank of clouds and there was the earth right beneath him in the falling rain. And there, also just below, was the hangar, with strong searchlights shining up against the clouds, and many men standing around, waiting for Zep to come home.

The Commander and his crew had all been expecting the big Dirigible to crash them against the ground any minute. When they saw that he had brought them home instead, what a wonderful feeling it gave them!

Zep was still sinking down

ZEPPELIN

THERE, JUST BELOW, WAS THE HANGAR

slowly, and without remembering that the steering apparatus had refused to work a while before, the Commander began to steer Zep.

"Why, it works all right now!" the officer cried suddenly. "What in the world could have been wrong with it? And how did we get back here when I thought all the time we were drifting farther from home?"

"Perhaps Zep knew the way home better than we did," said one of the men.

"It almost looks that way," agreed the Commander.

Then everybody became so busy getting Zep down into the hangar that he had no time to think any more about the matter. The Commander guided Zep slowly down toward the ground until he came close enough to drop ropes over to the men be-low. Catching hold of the ropes, the men on the ground pulled the big Dirigible down to them. The motors were shut off, and the propellers stopped. Then the men walked slowly through the big doors until they had Zep all safe and sound in his hangar once more.

And there, when he listened to the storm beating so hard against the big hangar, Zep was glad that he had been stubborn and had found the way home, at last.

"WHAT IS SO FUNNY—HO-HO!" SNORTED THE BIG ENGINE

The Sad Little Switch Engine

WHEN Choo-choo, the little Switch Engine, was brand-new, he was very happy, indeed. He ran about all day long, thinking what a big, strong Locomotive he would be when he grew up.

At first, Choo-choo worked in the railroad yard of a large city, where there were many, many tracks running along side by side. Here and there were places where the tracks crossed over and ran into one another.

These were called "switches." They had been built so that a train on one track could be made to cross over onto another track whenever one of the men pulled the right levers. The men who pulled the levers that made the cars go from one track to another were called switchmen.

Choo-choo worked for many, many days in the big railroad yard, and he was happy all the time. He took parts of the long trains of freight cars that came into the big city, and pushed first one freight car and then another

[47]

onto different tracks over the switches. In this way all the cars of the big trains were sorted out. The freight cars which were to go in one direction were ready on one track. Those which were to go in another direction were ready on another track. Then a big, strong, puffing Freight Locomotive would fasten himself to each line of cars, and away they all would go to some distant city.

Choo-choo always felt very proud of himself when he saw a big Freight Engine pulling a train out of the railroad yard.

"If it were not for me, he wouldn't find cars all ready for him to take out," the happy little Switch Engine would say to himself.

Then Choo-choo began to dream of the time when he would grow up. At first he decided that he would be a big, strong, Freight Locomotive which could pull long trains from one big city to another. But finally he began to wonder if it would not be more fun to grow up into a fine big Passenger Locomotive, instead.

Over at the edge of the railroad yard were several long, straight tracks which ran on and on, farther than anyone could see. These were the "main lines" which stretched for many, many miles to other big cities. Only trains bound for far-away cities were allowed to use these tracks.

Every day long Passenger Trains, carrying people instead of freight, would rush by on the main lines so fast that Choo-choo never even had a chance to say "How - do - you - do!" Sometimes he would call, "Toot-toot!" to them with his little whistle. And sometimes the big Locomotives would answer with a single "Toot!" from their big whistles. But it was a long time before he ever had a chance to talk with one of the big Passenger Locomotives.

It all happened one day when Choo-choo went over to the roundhouse to have a little leak in his boiler fixed. A fine big Passenger Engine stood beside him on the track in the roundhouse, and at first Choo-choo felt a little bashful. But the big Locomotive was very kind and soon he was telling the little Switch Engine all about the far cities he had been to, and how fast he could run.

"Do you think a Passenger Locomotive is more important than a big Freight Locomotive?" Choo-choo asked.

"My goodness, yes!" said the

CHOO-CHOO FELT VERY PROUD WHEN HE SAW A BIG FREIGHT ENGINE

big Passenger Engine. "Of course it is. Why else does a Freight Train always have to switch onto a sidetrack to let a Passenger Train go by, if the Passenger Train isn't the more important?"

"That's just what I thought," agreed Choo-choo, breathlessly. "That's just why I have decided that when I grow up, I shall be a Passenger Locomotive like you, instead of being a Freight Locomotive."

"When you grow up!" cried the big Passenger Engine, so surprised at what he had heard that he hardly knew what to say. And then, all at once, he began to laugh and laugh as though he had just heard the funniest joke in the world.

Choo-choo listened to his laughter. "What is so funny about that?" he asked.

"What is so funny — ho- ho!" snorted the big Engine. "Why, you little simpleton, people and dogs grow up, but a Locomotive always stays as he is made. Who ever heard of one growing up? The very idea! I'm ashamed of you for being so very simple."

And then he laughed until it seemed to Choo-choo that he would never stop.

Poor little Choo-choo had always been happy before, but now he became sad. He did not do his work well, and the Yardmaster thought that something was wrong inside him. He sent Choo-choo away to the roundhouse and asked the Locomotive Doctors there to make him well again.

The Doctors at the roundhouse packed and pounded him. They twisted all his bolts and tightened up his rivets. But they could not make him feel any bet-

THE DOCTORS AT THE ROUNDHOUSE PACKED AND POUNDED HIM

ter. When they had finished, Choo-choo behaved just as badly as before, because he could no longer dream of growing up.

He did his work so poorly that the Yardmaster in the big railroad yard finally asked for another Switch Engine to take Choo-choo's place. The new Switch Engine came and was given the work which Choo-choo had always done. And poor little Choo-choo stood on a side-track near the roundhouse, all alone and with nothing at all to do. But he did not care much what happened to him, now that he knew he could never grow up into a big Locomotive.

One day a new Engineer and Fireman approached Choo-choo as he stood sadly on the side-track. The Fireman once more built a fire in the little Switch Engine, and the Engineer walked all around him, squirting oil into him here and there with a big oil can. As soon as the fire had made steam in his boiler, the Engineer told the Fireman to ring the bell. Then little Choo-choo was backed away off the sidetrack. He wondered what they were going to do with him now, but he really didn't care very much, because he was so sad.

They filled his tender with coal, as much as he could carry,

and they gave him all the water that he could drink. Then the Engineer looked again at a piece of paper, to make sure he had his orders right.

"We can make it all the way without having to sidetrack," he told the Fireman, "if only this little old teapot gives us no trouble."

Choo-choo wondered what the Engineer meant. Then he realized that he, Choo-choo, was being called a little old teapot!

"The very idea!" he said to himself, becoming quite angry. "I'll just show them that I am as good as any other Locomotive. A little old teapot, indeed!"

And because he was angry, he forgot all about being sad for a while and began to work as well as he had ever done.

When he had been given as much coal and water as he could take, Choo-choo was run out on-

THE ENGINEER OPENED THE THROTTLE WIDE

to the main-line tracks. The Engineer opened the throttle wide and the little Switch Engine began to run as fast as he could—faster than he had ever run at any other time before.

He ran past the roundhouse. He ran through the big railroad yard where he used to push and pull freight cars around all day. There he saw the new Switch Engine, and he whistled to him, "Too-too-o-oot!" just as a big Locomotive would have done.

The first thing he knew, Choo-choo was out in the open country. His little heavy wheels turned so fast that they looked like tops spinning along on their sides. And suddenly, Choo-choo found that he was no longer sad. For he was speeding along the main line, just like one of the big Locomotives.

"I don't know where they are taking me," he laughed to himself, "but this is wonderful."

As he went along, he listened

to what the Engineer and Fireman were saying to each other, and before long he found out the reason for this trip. Some town along the railroad needed a Switch Engine in its little rail-

HE COUPLED ON THE LONG TRAIN OF BRIGHT, SHINY PASSENGER COACHES

road yard. Since Choo-choo no longer seemed able to do the hard work in the big yard in the city, he was being sent to the smaller town.

Choo-choo became unhappy when he thought of leaving the big city. But he quickly smiled again when he saw how fast he could make the fields and woods whiz by. He tooted his whistle for crossings. He ran past little railroad stations just as though he were a big Passenger Engine pulling a fine limited train.

After he had gone along for several hours, the Engineer began to slow him down a little as they neared the edge of a town.

"This is our stop, Ben," he said to the Fireman, and Choo-choo knew that he was coming into his new home.

At the little railroad station, the Engineer pulled Choo-choo onto a sidetrack and stopped him. Then he walked over to the station to let the operator know that Choo-choo had arrived. In a few moments, the Engineer came running back, waving a sheet of paper as he ran.

pull Number 10 so far without blowing off a couple of cylinder heads, itself?" asked the Fireman anxiously.

"If it runs as well after we pick up Number 10 as it did coming

THE LITTLE SWITCH ENGINE BEGAN TO GO FASTER AND FASTER

"Number 10 is laid up at the next town," he called to the Fireman. "Its Engine has blown both cylinder heads and is dead on the track. We are to sidetrack the dead Engine and then pull the train on into the city. We can get it there sooner than they can send a new Engine out here."

"But will this little old teapot

here, we'll make it fine," said the Engineer.

They turned Choo-choo around so that he could run backwards along the main line to the next town, where Train Number 10 and its big crippled Locomotive stood waiting.

Choo-choo could hardly believe what he had heard. Was it

really true that he was going to pull a fine train into the city, just like a big Locomotive?

He was even more surprised when at last he came to the spot where Number 10 stood waiting. He saw that the crippled Engine was none other than the fine big Passenger Engine which had stood beside him in the round-house and had laughed at him so hard. Choo-choo didn't want to make the poor fellow feel any worse, but he just couldn't help saying, "I really must be grow-ing up, after all, since they send me to pull your train in."

The crippled Locomotive did not laugh at him this time.

"Perhaps you are," he said. "You'll show yourself to be a real Locomotive if you will get my train into the city without losing any more time. Your little wheels make you rather slow, but try to do your best."

Choo-choo promised, very proud that the other should talk to him in such a grown-up way. First, he pulled the big, crippled Locomotive to a sidetrack out of the way. Next, he coupled on the long train of bright, shiny passenger coaches and began pulling it toward the big city.

The train was heavy, but not nearly as hard to pull as some of the long strings of freight cars which Choo-choo had pulled in the big railroad yard. The little Switch Engine did not mind the work at all. He began to go faster and faster. He wanted to show the big crippled Locomotive that he really was growing up. His Engineer opened the throttle wide, and away he sped.

At last he came once more to the city; he whizzed through the big railroad yard and past the roundhouse. Finally, under the great train shed of the station,

Choo-choo's Engineer stopped him. As the passengers began to get out of the coaches, Choo-choo was cut loose from the train. He rolled on down through the train shed and was switched onto another track, so that he could go back to the roundhouse.

At the roundhouse, the Engineer and the Fireman told what a fine Engine he was. They spoke so well of him that he was given his old work to do in the big railroad yard. No one ever had any fault to find with him again, because Choo-choo was happy now. He knew that although he was only a little Switch Engine and could never be anything else, yet once he had been grown up enough to pull a fine Passenger Engine and its long train of cars.

The Tale of Fanny Blowhard

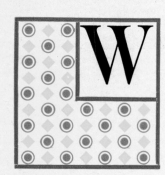 **W**HEN the late spring days began to turn quite warm and everyone could see that summer was very near, the Man looked about his office, rubbing his damp forehead with his handkerchief.

"I must have a good Electric Fan put in my office here," he said to himself. "It can blow on me all the time and keep me cool during the hot summer weather." For the Man was quite fat and he grew hot easily.

A few days later, he went out and bought himself a fine, big Electric Fan. That afternoon some electricians came and fastened it tightly to the office wall. Then they ran wires to it so that it would have plenty of electricity to make it go. When the Man came in and saw his new Fan, he was very much pleased that he had bought it.

"What a good-looking Fan it is!" he said. "I wonder how well it works."

He turned a switch and started the Fan going. As its motor began to whir and its blades began to spin, it gently blew out upon him a soft, cooling little breeze. It twisted and turned itself slowly as it ran, first to one side and then to the other, sending out its cooling breeze in every direction.

"Ah, a very fine Fan, indeed!" said the Man, much pleased. He thought of how cool it would keep him during the hot summer days to come.

Because her new master liked her so much, Fanny Blowhard—which was the Electric Fan's name—felt very happy. But when the Man had finished his day's work and had gone home, the Electric Fan began to discover that she really hadn't found such a pleasant new home, after all.

"Dear me, what a dreadful creature this new Fan is," growled the big Desk at which the Man always sat to do his work. "Now I suppose I shall have dust blown over me all of the time, and all my papers will be blown and scattered every-where around."

"My papers are certain to be blown about much worse than yours," said the Filing Cabinet, "because I have so many more of them."

"She will hum so loudly that no one will hear a word over me!" squealed the Telephone.

"She'll be blowing my trash all over the office!" cried the Wastebasket.

And all the other things in the office joined with those that had already spoken in being very rude to the new Electric Fan.

"Oh, dear me!" laughed Fanny Blowhard, for she thought that they were all just teasing her. "Come, now, stop your joking. Let's get acquainted with one another in the right way."

"COME, NOW, STOP YOUR JOKING"

"Joking!" exclaimed the big Desk. "I'm sure that I mean every word I say about your being a not - very - nice - person to have around our office."

"Joking!" cried the Filing Cabinet. "Why, the very idea! I was never more serious in my life!"

And all the other things around the office began laughing very rudely, also.

"Oh, come, come!" said Fanny at last, trying her hardest not to become angry. "I'm to be fastened to the wall here for a long, long time, and it will be so much nicer if we can all be friends."

"Friends! Humph!" snorted the Telephone. "As if any respectable piece of office equipment could be friends with a whizzing, whirring, humming nuisance like you!"

"JOKING!" EXCLAIMED THE DESK. "I'M SURE I MEAN EVERY WORD I SAY"

"Friends! Ha-ha!" laughed the Wastebasket. And "Ha-ha!" laughed all the others. The Filing Cabinet shook so hard that his filing sections flew open and all his cards and papers could be seen. The Typewriter laughed so hard that she got her keys all twisted up and couldn't have written a word then if she had had to. And the big Desk chuckled so mightily that his drawer locks burst open and all kinds of papers and pens began sticking their heads out of the drawers to see what was happening.

By this time the Electric Fan was really angry. She had done her best to keep a quarrel from starting, but everyone had been so unmannerly to her that she could be peaceful no longer.

"My name is Fanny Blowhard," she called to them all. "Now you shall see how well I am named!"

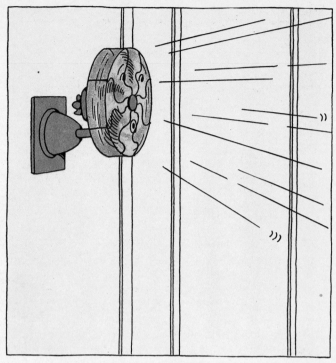

SHE TURNED HERSELF ON, FULL POWER

Suddenly she turned herself on, full power, and began to whiz and whir just as hard as electricity could possibly make her.

"H-u-m-mm-m-M-MMM!" came the rising sound of her motor. When it got to turning its very hardest, her broad fan blades stirred the air into a mighty wind that whirled about the office.

"Oh, stop, stop!" cried the Filing Cabinet. "You are blowing away all my nicely filed papers and cards!"

HER BROAD FAN BLADES STIRRED THE AIR INTO A MIGHTY WIND

But the Electric Fan did not stop. She was so angry that she blew all the papers out of the Filing Cabinet and sent them fluttering about the office like big flakes of snow in a blizzard. And then she turned to the Desk and blew everything off his top and many things out of the Desk drawers. "Stop, please do, Fanny!"

begged the Desk. "You're blowing all my things away."

But Fanny did not stop. She turned over the Wastebasket and blew out his trash and mixed it with the other papers flying about the office. She upset the Telephone and made him break his receiver when he fell on the hard floor. She whirled the big Desk Chair around and around, until she twisted him right out of his base and he tumbled onto the middle of the floor. She tangled up the keys of the Typewriter worse than ever, so that the Typewriter would have to be fixed again before she could write another word.

At last, after Fanny had blown about everything that could be blown, she became less angry. And when she saw what a terrible mix-up she had made in the office, she felt too ashamed to be angry any more.

"Oh, I'm so sorry!" she said, as she stopped her motor and looked about the office. Papers were scattered everywhere, over the floor and over the furniture. It looked as if a sudden snowfall had settled down in heavy drifts. The Filing Cabinet was empty and ready to shed tears. All the papers and pens and pencils that belonged to the Desk were scattered about in every direction. The Chair had been twisted in two, the Telephone had fallen to the floor, and everything else was in dreadful shape.

"Oh, I'm so sorry!" said the Electric Fan again. "I was so angry I didn't think of what I was doing."

"That's all right," rumbled the big Desk. "We brought it all upon ourselves by being rude to you. We deserve all we got."

"Indeed we do," groaned the Filing Cabinet. "If only I hadn't been rude, I needn't have lost all my papers."

All the other office things then began to tell Fanny that she had done nothing more than any-one else would have done in her place and that they were really to blame for the whole thing. This made the Electric Fan feel both glad and sorry at the same time, and she hardly knew what to do or say.

"You're all so nice, after all," she said to them. "I promise never to blow your papers away again, or to blow dust on you, or to hum too loudly, or to do anything else that might trouble you."

"And we'll never be rude to you again," said all the office things. "We'll all be good friends together and never quarrel." And so the new Electric Fan found a happy home after all.

When the Man saw his office the next morning, he thought that thieves had broken in and thrown everything around in their search for money. The Police came, and soon they were all hunting for burglars. No one ever thought about the Electric Fan and the other office things having caused all the confusion while they were quarreling with one another!

SOON THE ELEVATOR WAS ALL READY TO VENTURE OUT ON THE STREETS

The Runaway Elevator

"UP AND down! Up and down!" the Elevator said to himself. "I am tired of going up and down all day long, day after day. I wonder how it would seem to go sidewise for a while."

He was not a very big Elevator, because the building he was in was not very big. The building was old, also, and the Elevator had been there for a long, long time.

Just beside him, at the very back of the building, was a great wide door where the janitor sometimes unloaded boxes and other things. The building was so small that the Elevator had to carry up these boxes as well as people, and this often made him go up and down many times at night, after everybody had gone home.

One day a little red Automobile Truck backed up to the big door beside the Elevator, so that the boxes he carried could be unloaded.

"Hello, there, Mr. Up-and-

Down," cried the Truck. "How nice it must be to go up high, as you do, and then drop down again. It must be lots of fun."

"Oh, it was rather good sport at first," said the Elevator. "But I have gone up and down so many times that it has become very tiresome. I wish that I could run along on the level ground for a while, as you do."

"And I wish that I could go up and down for a while, like you," said the little red Truck. "The only time that I ever go up and down is when I hit a great big bump in the street. What keeps you from falling when you get up so high, Mr. Up-and-Down?"

"Oh, I have strong wire cables fastened to me and weights to help balance me. Then there is an electric motor in the basement that works hard to pull me up and down," ex-

plained the Elevator. "Of course, if the cables should ever break, then I might come down—ker-plunk!"

"It must be lots of fun, going up so high," said the little red Truck. "How high do you go, Mr. Up-and-Down?"

"I go to the top of this building," said the Elevator.

"To the very top?" cried the Truck.

"Oh, yes," said the Elevator.

"I wish that I could take your place for a while," said the little red Truck. "I would like to go up and down more than anything else I can think of."

"And I wish I could take your place," sighed the Elevator. "I think it would be great fun to do something different."

"I might lend you my wheels," offered the little Truck, generously.

"And I might lend you my

cables and weights," said the Elevator.

"What fun it would be if we

"My janitor, the night watchman, always goes to sleep up on the fourth floor, after he finishes

"MY JANITOR ALWAYS GOES TO SLEEP AFTER HE FINISHES HIS SWEEPING"

could just change places for a little while!" cried the little red Truck.

"Let's do it!" suggested the Elevator.

"Let's do it tonight, after everyone has gone home," said the Truck.

his sweeping," said the Elevator. "If you will come here then, we can trade places for a while, and no one will know anything about it. Won't that be great?"

"Wonderful!" cried the jolly little Truck.

"I'll look for you, then, after

the big whistle blows at nine o'clock," said the Elevator.

And that is the way it came about that the Elevator and the little red Automobile Truck traded places for a while that night and the Elevator ran away to see the world.

After the big whistle blew at nine o'clock, the little Truck slipped out of his shed without anyone's seeing him and rolled along softly to the big door where the Elevator was waiting.

"Just come right on in, through the big door, Mr. Truck," said the Elevator. "My janitor is sound asleep on the fourth floor."

So the jolly red Truck rolled right on into the building. He loaned his wheels to the Elevator, and the Elevator loaned the Truck his cables and weights and helped him to get settled comfortably in the elevator shaft.

"I have told the Motor in the basement all about you," said the Elevator, "and he is ready to pull you up and down a few times right away, just to let you know how it feels. Then, after that, you must not go unless the janitor rides along with you."

The Elevator called down to the Motor in the basement, and the Motor began to wind up the long cables that were fastened to the little red Truck. The little Truck began to shoot up the elevator shaft. He kept on going up and up, until at last he was at the very top of the building.

The Motor stopped whirring for a moment, and then it started again, unwinding all the long cables it had just wound up. As it did so, it let the little red Truck drop back down the elevator shaft until he was once more at the ground floor.

"Whee-e-ee!" cried the little

Truck. "I am so thrilled. I don't see how you could ever get tired of doing this, Mr. Up-and-Down."

"It's because I have done it so many times, Mr. Truck," the Elevator explained. "Now the Motor will pull you up and down three more times. Then I shall roll along on your wonderful wheels and see how the world looks from the level ground."

The little red Truck was pulled up to the very top of the building three more times and let down again each time. And every time that he went up and down, he became more thrilled than ever, although riding in such a funny manner did make him a little dizzy.

After he had come down the last time, he remembered that it was dark outside.

"You must have lights so that you can see the road and no one will run into you," he told the Elevator. "Just a moment, and I will lend you my lamps. I had better give you my horn, as well. You can toot it to make people get out of your way."

Soon the Elevator was all ready to venture out on the level streets on the Truck's four wonderful wheels. Before he left, he had the Motor in the basement pull the little red Truck up to the fourth floor, where the janitor was asleep.

"I don't think he will wake up before I get back," the Elevator told the Truck. "But you had better stay there, because if he does wake up, he will be very angry if he has to walk downstairs."

Then the Elevator rolled out through the big door on his four borrowed wheels and on through the dark alley until he came to a street. He was so used to going up and down all the time that being able to move about in a different way seemed the most wonderful thing in the world.

He was a very queer-looking object, indeed. He was just a big square cage, running along on four wheels, with bright lights in front to show him the way to go and a red light behind so that no one would run into him.

"What great fun this is!" the Elevator said to himself, as he stopped for a moment at the end of the alley. "I wonder where all the people are?"

As he looked, he saw that there were many bright lights far down at one end of the street. He turned and ran along on his four wheels toward them.

He began to see more and more people as he rolled down the street. Presently he was right in among a crowd of automobiles and street cars. There were so many lights all around him that it was almost as bright as day, and there were more people than the Elevator had ever seen before at one time.

He began to be worried when he noticed everybody stopping and staring at him.

"Why do they look at me so strangely?" he asked himself. "I am bothering no one. And surely I do not look strange, for I have wheels and lights and a horn just like these automobiles around me."

But the people stared harder than ever, and they began to crowd closely around the Elevator. He had to honk his horn loudly to make them get out of the way.

"Just look at the cage on wheels!" some one called.

"Where are the animals that were in the cage?" asked some one else, thinking the Elevator might be an empty circus cage that had become lost.

"There is no one in it to run it!" a woman cried.

"It looks just like an elevator," said a man.

"It is an elevator," exclaimed another.

Because they were all curious and wanted to see the queer sight the crowd began to push more closely about the poor Elevator. Soon there were so many people around him that all the automobiles and street cars had to stop. They began a dreadful honking of horns and clanging of gongs. The Elevator grew more nervous than ever.

He was really beginning to be frightened. The crowd was so thick that he feared he would never get back to his building again. He wondered what the little red Truck would do in case he never came back—the poor little Truck, hanging in an elevator shaft, without any wheels or lights or horn!

He began to honk his horn again. Then he began to push forward against the crowd. He bumped a fat man so hard that the man said, "Oomp!" and got out of his way in a hurry. And he ran over the toes of a red-headed boy who was about to climb onto him, so that the boy got out of his way, also.

At last, he was able to push out of the crowd. He ran along as fast as his four wheels would carry him, until he came to a part of town where it was dark and where there were no people or automobiles or street cars to be seen. There he stopped and rested for a while.

It took him a long time to find his way back to his little old building. At last, when he did get back home, he was so tired

HE BUMPED A BIG FAT MAN SO HARD THE MAN SAID, "OOMP!"

that he felt he never wanted to travel on the level streets again. Going up and down in his cozy elevator shaft was much more pleasant.

When he rolled through the big open door, he saw that the little red Truck was there on the ground floor, instead of up at the fourth floor where he had been left.

"What has happened, Mr. Truck?" asked the Elevator, anxiously.

The little red Truck laughed.

"Why, the janitor woke up and came to the shaft. He jumped in me, and I started down with him before he woke up enough to notice that I had changed places with you. When he saw what a funny Elevator I was, he began to yell loudly about being bewitched. When I got him down here, he jumped out and ran away."

The Elevator felt relieved.

"Oh, well, that is not so bad," he said. "I didn't like him very much, anyhow. Perhaps now I shall get a nicer janitor."

"I hope you had a good time," said the little red Truck. "I have enjoyed going up and down, but really I am quite ready to trade back again. It made me quite dizzy, hanging there all that time so far from the ground. I don't see how you stand it, Mr. Up-and-Down."

"And I don't see how you stand being out on the crowded streets, Mr. Truck," said the Elevator. "I am sure that I never want to try it again."

Then the Elevator gave back the four wheels and the lights and the horn which he had borrowed from the little red Truck. And the Truck gave back the Elevator's weights and cables. They both said good night, and the jolly little red Truck rolled away home, while the Elevator went up and down a few times to see that everything was working all right. It seemed to him that going up and down was the most pleasant thing he could imagine.

Never again did the Elevator want to run away. It always made him happy to think that no crowd of unmannerly people could get in his way as long as he stayed safely in his shaft in the little old building.

The Plane That Tried to Fly to the Sun

WHEN the little Airplane was being put together, his builders named him Eagle, because they thought that he would be able to fly like an eagle. Young Mack, his pilot, was very, very proud of the new Airplane.

"I have a feeling," he told the other men at the big flying field, "that Eagle is going to fly higher and faster than any plane this field has ever known. Perhaps he will even break a few records."

It pleased Eagle very much to hear Young Mack say this. He was anxious to fly high in the air, and he was glad that Young Mack had been chosen to fly him.

The morning came when the pilot was to take Eagle up for the first time, to test him out. All the other flyers and the workers at the big field had gathered about to see how the new Plane would act in the air.

Eagle's motor was started and ran with a soft, low hum until it was all warmed up. Then Young Mack came out, dressed in heavy flying clothes which would keep him warm when he flew high up in the air. Young Mack climbed into the little cockpit, the place in an Airplane where the flyer sits. He wore a parachute strapped to his back, in case Eagle should fall down.

At the thought of flying for the first time, Eagle was so excited that he could hardly wait for his motor to warm up. He wanted to go up, up, up, higher and higher in the sky, until people and houses down on the ground became too small to be seen.

Young Mack settled himself in the cockpit. He looked at all the instruments and dials and gauges in front of him to make sure that everything about Eagle was all right. Then the men on the ground beside the little Plane pulled away the big blocks which had kept Eagle from running forward while his motor was warming up. Young Mack turned on more gas so that Eagle's motor roared loudly and his propeller blew sand and dirt backward. Then the little Airplane sprang forward and ran very fast on the ground for a short distance.

Suddenly, he seemed to leap

HE SETTLED HIMSELF IN THE COCKPIT

right up into the air. He felt so happy, as soon as he found himself off the ground, that he kept on going up and up and up, turning in a wide circle as he climbed. His path was just like a big corkscrew.

The people on the field below watched Eagle with amazement.

"What a wonderful take-off," said one. "He just jumped up into the air."

"And look at him climb!" cried another.

Everybody said such nice things about Eagle that he might have been spoiled if he had heard them. Eagle, however, could not hear what was being said, and even if he could, would not have paid much attention. For he felt that at last he was doing the thing he had been made for. He was going up and up in the sky.

Eagle could no longer see the people on the ground and still he climbed. And now he was flying so high that the air was becoming thin. Young Mack found it hard to breathe, and Eagle could scarcely get enough air to mix with the gasoline in his carburetor. But the Airplane was not yet ready to go back down to earth. He had seen something high above the clouds through which he had climbed — something so strange and wonderful that he wanted to keep on flying until he reached it.

Eagle had seen the sun, but because he was such a very new Plane, he did not know what it was. He thought that it was just a great warm yellow ball hung up very high in the sky, and he climbed to get closer to it.

At last, the air grew so thin and cold that Young Mack had to turn the little Plane back toward the earth. And Eagle, who had felt sure a moment ago that he would be able to reach the bright golden ball of the sun, grew rather sad. He glided down and down and down, until at last the flying field could be seen again.

As Young Mack and Eagle came nearer and nearer the earth, the crowd of people waiting for them at the big field seemed to

"IT WAS A PERFECT TEST FLIGHT," HE TOLD THE MEN WHO CROWDED ABOUT

grow larger and larger. At last they were just above the field, and then Eagle settled down. Light as a feather, he ran along on his two rubber-tired wheels and the little runner at his back, called the tail skid, toward the place from which he had started.

Young Mack stopped the motor and climbed out of the cockpit, all stiff from the cold of the upper air, but happy.

"It was a perfect test flight," he told the men on the field who crowded about him to ask all sorts of questions. "Eagle will break every record that has ever been made the next time we go up. After we put in oxygen tanks and put a supercharger on the motor, the thin air above cannot stop us."

Then Eagle knew that Young Mack had just been testing him out this time and that soon he would have another chance to fly higher than ever. "Next time," he thought, "I shall fly to the yellow ball and see just what it is before Young Mack turns me back to earth."

So Eagle was pushed into his

AS HE STARTED UP THROUGH THE AIR, THE PLANE FELT VERY HAPPY

hangar, and then the men began to work on him to make him ready for his next flight into the upper air. They put in oxygen tanks so that Young Mack would be able to breathe when the air got too thin. Also, they put a supercharger on the motor so that Eagle would have enough air to breathe, too.

Any gasoline motor, you know, has to have air to breathe through its carburetor, just like a human being or animal, and if it has no air, it will not run. The supercharger which was put on Eagle's motor was a piece of machinery that would gather thin air from the upper sky and pump it fast through Eagle's carburetor. Then his motor could go on running as well in the thin air as down nearer the earth.

The air which we breathe is all around the world just like a blanket. It is heaviest and thick-

ABOVE HIM WAS THE YELLOW BALL

est down near the sea. Then, as one climbs up a high mountain, the air begins to get thinner and lighter, so that it becomes harder to breathe. And when one flies high into the sky, as Young Mack and Eagle had done, the air becomes still thinner and lighter. It becomes colder, also, until it is much colder than in the coldest winter — colder than air ever is at the North Pole.

Young Mack knew this, and that was why he had all these things done to Eagle. For Young Mack wanted to fly higher up in the sky than any man had ever flown before.

At last Eagle was all ready to go. One bright morning, he was rolled out of his hangar onto the flying field. His motor was started and left running slowly until it was warmed up. Young Mack came out to him then, looking like a great woolly bear. He was wearing many warm furs to keep him from freezing up above. He climbed into the little cockpit, and then the blocks were removed.

Eagle's motor began to roar. The little Plane leaped forward as he had done before and then jumped into the air. Almost above him, it seemed, was the great round yellow ball. As he started up through the air, the little Plane felt very happy.

"Now," he said to himself, "I shall fly on and on, until I can see just what that wonderful golden thing is."

So he flew up and up and up, higher and higher all the time, making his corkscrew path through the air. But no matter

AT LAST THEY COULD SEE THE FIELD FROM WHICH THEY HAD STARTED

how high he went, he never seemed to come any nearer the yellow ball. It always looked just as far away as it had when he started. The air became so thin and cold as Eagle climbed that he knew he was far above the spot where Young Mack had turned him back to earth before. His motor coughed and spit a little, but the supercharger gave him air enough to breathe.

Eagle soon found that in the thinner air he could not fly upward as fast as he had been doing. An Airplane, you know, flies because its motor and propeller push the air backward so fast that the Plane is pulled forward, and as it goes forward, its wings grip the air and lift it upward. When the air grew so thin, Eagle's motor could not make him go forward as fast nor could his wings lift him as high as they had done nearer the earth. But

DOWN AND DOWN THEY WENT

still Eagle climbed, although he went more and more slowly.

"I shall never be able to see what that great round yellow ball looks like," Eagle said sadly to himself. "This air is getting so thin that I can't fly up much farther."

Still his motor roared on, and his propeller whirled around. He kept climbing, climbing, just a very little bit now, but still flying a little higher all the time.

And Young Mack, back in the closed cockpit, was so cold, even through all his warm furs, that he was nearly frozen. But he would not turn back toward the earth.

"Go on, little Eagle," he whispered. "I'll not turn you back until you get so high that you cannot climb another inch."

Eagle heard Young Mack, and he climbed a little higher, though it was dreadfully hard work. At last he was so high that he could not rise another inch. The air had become so thin that when he would climb up a little bit, he would drop back the next instant. He tried and tried to fly nearer to the big round yellow sun, but he couldn't do it.

"That's all, little Eagle," whispered Young Mack through lips that were almost frozen. "That's as far as we can go. And now we must drop back to earth and tell them all about it."

Then Eagle turned back toward the earth and glided down, making another corkscrew path through the thin air. He felt sad because he had not been able to fly to the sun.

"Perhaps next time I shall make it," he said to himself. But really, he felt sure that he had flown this time as high as he could ever go.

Young Mack and Eagle were so far above the earth that nothing could be seen of it for a long, long time except some fleecy white clouds that shadowed it. Then, as they glided down, they passed through the clouds and could see far below them little threads that were great rivers

AND THEN WHAT A LOT OF EXCITEMENT THERE WAS!

and little spots of color that were big cities.

Down and down they went, getting closer and closer to the earth. And as they came nearer, all the things on the ground seemed to grow larger, until at last they could see the big flying field from which they had started. There they saw a crowd of people waiting for them to land.

When, at last, they were only a little above the earth, Eagle settled down and ran along on the ground until he was near the hangars where all the people stood.

And then what a lot of excitement there was! The men lifted Young Mack out of the cockpit, for he was still so cold and stiff that he could not climb out by himself. Other men with cameras took pictures of him and of little Eagle. And still other

men, who were high officers of the flying field, lifted a little black instrument out of the place where it had been fastened to Eagle.

This was a special instrument called a barograph, and it had written down inside it the whole story of the flight. It showed with little thin lines just how high above the earth Eagle and Young Mack had gone.

The men opened up the barograph, and then they began to call out in great excitement. And everybody that heard them began to cheer as loudly as he could.

Young Mack and Eagle had flown higher into the sky than any other man or Airplane had ever gone! They had set a new record!

Everybody was cheering and laughing and so happy that Eagle could no longer be sad, even though he had not flown to the sun. Since he had climbed nearer to it than any other Airplane, he began to feel satisfied. When the men pushed him into his hangar again, Eagle forgot his dream of flying to the sun and began to dream, instead, of other wonderful flights he and Young Mack would make.

"THIS IS SUCH A NICE DAY, LET'S TAKE A LONG RIDE"

The Lazy Automobile

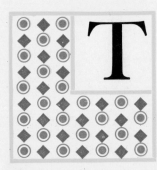THERE once was a little Automobile, named Chuffer, who had grown lazy. As long as he had been new and strong, he had enjoyed carrying people everywhere they wanted to go. But one day, when he stopped to think of all the work he had done, he began to feel tired. Then he became lazy, and he soon grew so lazy that he didn't want to work at all.

His master's name was Mr. Smiggles. Chuffer didn't like Mr. Smiggles because he made him work, and he tried to think of a way to get even.

"Some day he'll be sorry that he makes me work so hard," Chuffer said to himself many times. "The very idea, a big, healthy man like him wanting to ride every place he goes!"

One Sunday afternoon, Mr. Smiggles said to Mrs. Smiggles, "This is such a nice day, let's take a long ride out into the country."

"Fine," said Mrs. Smiggles. "I'll call up Aunt Lucy and

Uncle Fred and ask them to go with us. And then I shall get the children ready."

So, while she was calling Aunt Lucy and Uncle Fred and dressing the children, Mr. Smiggles ran around the corner with the lazy Automobile to a gas station. There he filled Chuffer's tank with gasoline, gave him some oil, and pumped up all his tires. Then he drove back to get Mrs. Smiggles and the two Smiggles children.

"Uncle Fred and Aunt Lucy will be waiting for us," Mrs. Smiggles said as she and the children climbed into the lazy little Automobile.

Mr. Smiggles drove to Uncle Fred's house, and there were Uncle Fred and Aunt Lucy waiting for them. Two other people were waiting for them, also.

"Mr. and Mrs. Piffle came over just after you asked us to go," Aunt Lucy said. "So I asked them to come along with us."

Aunt Lucy climbed into the back of the lazy little Automobile. As she sat down, Chuffer gave a groan and cried to himself, "Oh, my poor springs!" For Aunt Lucy was very big and heavy.

Aunt Lucy took one of the Smiggles children on her broad lap, and Mrs. Smiggles took the other, and that made room for Mrs. Piffle to get in between them. Then Mr. Piffle and Uncle Fred got into the front seat with Mr. Smiggles.

They fitted in so tightly that Mr. Smiggles did not have very much room to drive; so he twisted and turned about in his seat until he pushed Uncle Fred and Mr. Piffle more tightly together than ever.

"All right," called Mr. Smig-

"ALL RIGHT," CALLED MR. SMIGGLES, "HERE WE GO!"

gles, "here we go!" And off they started in the lazy little Automobile.

"Oh, my goodness gracious!" groaned Chuffer, as he ran along on the smooth street. "What hard work this is! Just as soon as I find a good place, I shall stop and sleep a little while, to get rested."

So he rolled along until he arrived downtown, where there were high buildings. The streets were filled with other automobiles and street cars and people, and Mr. Smiggles made Chuffer go a little slower because of the crowds. Then, just at the busiest corner, a big Policeman blew his whistle and Mr. Smiggles had to make Chuffer stop very quickly.

Chuffer looked around and saw that he would have to wait a while before he could go on.

"This is a good place to take a little nap," he thought. And then, all at once, he went sound asleep.

Of course, when he went to sleep, his motor stopped running. This made Mr. Smiggles very nervous. He stepped on the starter, but the engine would not move. For, you see, the lazy little Automobile was asleep all over, and his engine could not start until he woke up.

The big Policeman blew his whistle again and motioned Mr. Smiggles to drive on. But Mr. Smiggles could not drive on. He just sat there and pressed his foot on the starter so that it turned over and over. But no matter how much it turned, it could not make Chuffer wake up.

"Choke your engine more," called Mrs. Smiggles from the back seat.

"No, don't choke it," called

THE CARS BEHIND HONKED THEIR HORNS LOUDER AND LOUDER

Aunt Lucy. "Just hold your spark back!"

"I think it would be better if you would choke it a great deal and hold your spark back, too," called Mrs. Piffle.

All the cars behind Chuffer, that wanted to pass him, began to honk their horns loudly. Mr. Smiggles became more nervous than ever.

"I shall have to get out and crank this thing!" he growled. He turned the crank as hard as he could, but even that didn't make the lazy little Automobile wake up.

The cars behind honked their horns louder and louder, until the big Policeman began to get angry, too. He walked over to Mr. Smiggles and said, "Why don't you start that thing and move it along?"

"IT WON'T START," GROANED MR. SMIGGLES, ALL OUT OF BREATH

"It won't start," groaned Mr. Smiggles, all out of breath.

"Well, climb back in," growled the big Policeman, "and I'll see if I can't make it start."

Mr. Smiggles got back into his seat, and the Policeman took hold of the crank and began to turn it. And because he was a big, strong Policeman, he whirled the crank around so fast and hard that it shook the lazy little Automobile from one end to the other and made him wake up and start running again.

"My goodness, but I am glad that is over," said Mr. Smiggles, as they rolled on down the street. "I hope nothing like that happens again."

"Then you shouldn't make me work so hard," the lazy little Automobile said to himself.

They rolled along and along, and all the time Chuffer was looking for another place to take a nap. They drove through the edge of the city and found themselves in the country on a fine, paved road. Chuffer didn't have to work very hard on this smooth pavement, so he didn't try to go to sleep again just yet.

"There are too many people on this road," said Mrs. Smiggles. "It doesn't seem like the real country."

"Let's turn off along some side road," said Aunt Lucy.

So, presently, when they came to a country road that led away from the smooth pavement, Mr. Smiggles turned onto it. It was harder for Chuffer to run on this road than it had been on the pavement, but still the lazy little Automobile could not find a good place to take a nap. So they drove along, and everyone enjoyed the quiet of the woods and fields they passed—everyone except Chuffer.

HE SAW A GREAT BLACK MUD PUDDLE

The road began to get a little rougher. Chuffer was afraid that his springs would break or that his old tires would burst, but he kept on rolling along. Presently, just ahead of him he saw a great black mud puddle. The puddle lay across the road from one side to the other, and it was very long.

"My goodness," Chuffer said to himself, "what a fine place this is to take a nap in!" He ran right on to the very middle of the puddle, and there he stopped dead still.

"Now," he laughed to himself, " they will all have to sit right here until I get ready to wake up, because they will be afraid to get out into the mud to disturb me." He settled down a little deeper in the puddle and fell sound asleep.

"This awful thing is dead again," groaned Mr. Smiggles.

AUNT LUCY FELL RIGHT INTO THE DEEPEST PART OF THE PUDDLE

He stepped on the starter, but it had gone to sleep, too, and would not make the motor turn over a single time.

"You'll have to get out and crank it," called fat Aunt Lucy from the back seat.

"You will just ruin your clothes," cried Mrs. Smiggles.

"Well," said Mr. Smiggles sadly, "it can't be helped. I'll have to try cranking it, mud or no mud."

He climbed out into the puddle and waded around in front of the lazy little Automobile. Mr. Smiggles cranked and cranked, splashing mud all over his Sunday clothes, but he couldn't make Chuffer wake up. When he could crank no more, Uncle Fred got down in the mud and tried. And when Uncle Fred grew tired, Mr. Piffle tried. But none of them was able to do a thing.

"This is the last time I ever go riding with you, George Henry Smiggles!" scolded Aunt Lucy.

"And I feel the same way about it," said Mrs. Piffle, sharply.

"It's going to get dark before long," snapped Mrs. Smiggles, "and we can't stay here all night. What are you going to do, Mr. Smiggles?"

"Well, we can't get this awful thing started again," replied Mr. Smiggles. "There's a trolley line to the city back along this road two or three miles. I guess you had better ride on the trolley to town. I shall stay here and you can send some one after me to tow me in."

"How are we ever going to get out in all this mud?" asked Mrs. Smiggles.

"The men are muddy, already," said Aunt Lucy. "They can carry us across."

So Mr. Smiggles and Uncle Fred carried the children across the puddle to the dry road. And then they came back and told Aunt Lucy they would carry her next. Aunt Lucy stood on the running board of the car. The men tried to pick her up and carry her. But she was so heavy, they let her slip a little, and then, first thing they knew—kersplash! —Aunt Lucy fell right into the deepest part of the puddle.

"If that's the way you do it," scolded Mrs. Smiggles, "you shan't carry me!" And she stepped out of the car into the mud.

"Nor me," snapped Mrs. Piffle. She stepped out, too. Both women waded haughtily through the mud and started down the road.

"George Henry Smiggles, if you ever get back home again," Mrs. Smiggles called back as she left, "don't you bring that awful car with you!"

"Something seems to have made her angry," remarked Mr. Smiggles.

"They all seem a little that way," said Uncle Fred and Mr. Piffle. "We had better hurry along with them. We'll send some one after you, so just wait here."

And then away went Uncle Fred and Mr. Piffle, leaving poor Mr. Smiggles alone with the lazy little Automobile.

It was after dark when a big, strong truck came to pull Mr. Smiggles and Chuffer out of the mudhole. It pulled them back to the city, and still the lazy little Automobile never woke up.

"Now, let's try to start it," said the Man who drove the big truck, when he had pulled Mr. Smiggles up to his garage. He tried to wake up Chuffer and make him run, but he couldn't.

By this time Mr. Smiggles was cold and hungry and angrier than ever. "That car isn't good for anything except the junk pile!" he cried.

"I'll give you five dollars for it," said the Garage Man.

"All right," said Mr. Smiggles. "I'm so tired of it that I never want to see it again."

So the Garage Man bought the Automobile from Mr. Smiggles for five dollars, and Mr. Smiggles took his five dollars and went home on a trolley car.

The next morning again the Garage Man tried to make Chuffer run, but the little Automobile was still too lazy to wake up. So the Garage Man tied him once more to the truck and pulled him out to a big open lot where hundreds and hundreds of Automobiles stood.

All these Automobiles were old and rusty. All had lost parts of their machinery, so that they could never run again. There the Garage Man and his helper began to take out Chuffer's engine and some of his other parts, and at last this woke him up.

"My goodness," he said to himself, when he looked around him. "Where is the mud puddle, and the Smiggles', and all the others? I don't remember this place."

THE GARAGE MAN AND HIS HELPER BEGAN TO TAKE OUT CHUFFER'S ENGINE

And then he noticed that two strange men were taking his engine out of him. "What in the world are they doing with me?" he wondered.

There was a rusty old Automobile beside him in the big lot, and Chuffer said to him, "What is this place and what are these men doing to me?"

"This," replied the Automobile, "is an Automobile graveyard. When an Automobile gets so lazy that he won't run any more, they bring him here and take out all his parts which are worth anything. Then they leave the rest of him to rust away."

When the lazy little Automobile heard this, he began to wish that he had not been quite so sleepy.

"Here, here!" he cried to the men. "I don't want to have my engine taken out. I'll never be lazy again, if you will just give me another chance."

But the men didn't hear a word he said. They went right on taking out his engine and his other parts. When they had everything that they wanted, the men drove away.

Poor little Chuffer looked around at the rusty old Automobile beside him, wanting to ask a great many questions. But the Automobile had gone back to sleep again. At last, because there was nothing else for him to do, the lazy little Automobile went to sleep, also. And he is probably sleeping yet. For what had happened to him is just what usually happens to Automobiles when they become so old and lazy that they will not run any more.

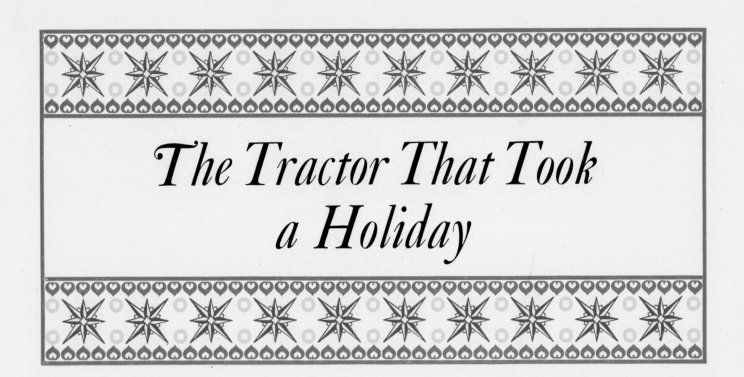

The Tractor That Took a Holiday

"CLANK, clank! chuff, chuff!" roared and rattled the big Tractor as he ran about doing his work on the farm where he lived. His motor puffed and snorted until he sounded like several automobiles running a race with one another. And as he moved along on his caterpillar tracks, he clanked and banged with such a great noise that he was called Rattler, which was a very good name for him, indeed.

Rattler worked very hard every day. He pulled the great Plows, whose sharp shares tore up the earth in the fields to make it ready for planting wheat and corn and other seeds. He dragged the bristly-toothed Harrows and heavy Rollers over the freshly plowed ground to break up the big clods and to smooth the dirt, so that the seeds would have a better bed in which to lie. And he pulled the Drills, or planting machines, which dropped the tiny seeds into the ground and covered them up in

RATTLER WOULD HAVE A GREAT TIME RUNNING A THRESHING MACHINE

the best way to make them sprout and grow into big plants.

When the wheat and oats were ripe in the summer sun, the big Tractor would clank through the bright fields pulling a great Binder. As he ran along, the keen knives of the Binder would cut quickly through the grain stalks. Then, as their heavy heads drooped, the Binder would catch them and tie them into bundles that were dropped here and there over the field.

For several days afterwards, Rattler would have a great time running a Threshing Machine with a big whirring belt. The Thresher would beat the wheat and oat grains from the straw and chaff. He would throw the golden straw up into a big stack and pour the bright clean grains into sacks. The wheat could then be taken to the mill to be ground into fine white flour for bread. The oats would be stored away for horse feed for the winter.

Since Rattler had many other tasks to do on the big farm, he worked very hard every day. He really didn't mind keeping busy all the time, except once in a while when he grew a little tired. Then he wished that he might have a whole day to himself with not a bit of work to do.

At last, one day in the fall, the big Tractor had his holiday! Mike, the Hired Man, who always rode on him and showed him what to do, drove Rattler into his shed one evening.

"Well, old fellow," he said, "you can have a whole day's rest tomorrow, with not a thing to do. We're all going to the Fair early in the morning, to be gone all day, and there'll be no work done. So rest up; for the next day we must get the big field ready for sowing wheat."

"How nice!" said Rattler to himself, when Mike had gone. "So I get a holiday tomorrow, do I? I'm very tired of working. I think I shall just stand in my shed and not even move."

And he went to sleep that night thinking of the fine holiday he would have, without a thing to do.

"YOU CAN HAVE A WHOLE DAY'S REST"

He tried to sleep late the next morning, but he couldn't do it. He was awake bright and early, just as usual, and he heard all the people of the farm leaving for the Fair. He began to feel lonesome and restless, which was no way to feel on a nice holiday. At last he could not stand being quiet any longer.

"I'll just roll along over to the big field and see where I'm going to start work tomorrow," he said to himself.

He felt much better as soon as he had started his motor and clanked out into the barnyard.

"Good morning, Mr. Rattler," a cheery voice greeted him as he roared out of his shed. "Where are you going so bright and early?"

When Rattler looked around he saw that it was the big Plow speaking to him. The Plow stood there, all ready to begin work the next day in the big field, and his sharp shares glittered in the sun.

"Good morning, Mr. Plow," answered Rattler. "I was feeling a little restless, with nothing to do. I thought I would just roll along over to the big field and see where we must work tomorrow morning."

"How interesting!" said the Plow. "May I come along with you?"

"Surely, Mr. Plow," replied Rattler, glad to have company. "Just hook yourself onto my drawbar, and I'll take you right along."

So the Plow hooked himself onto the big Tractor, and Rattler made his motor roar as together they began to clank on toward the big field.

But they had hardly started when another voice called, "Good morning, Mr. Rattler.

"GOOD MORNING, MR. RATTLER," A CHEERY VOICE GREETED HIM

Where are you taking Mr. Plow this fine, bright holiday?"

The big Tractor glanced around, and he saw the Harrow grinning at him with all his bristly teeth.

"Oh, good morning, Mr. Harrow," said Rattler. "Mr. Plow and I are tired of standing still with nothing to do. So we thought we would roll over to the big field and see where we have to start work tomorrow."

"Oh, but that will be fine," grinned the Harrow. "Please take me along with you."

"Very well," said Rattler, glad to have Mr. Harrow's company. "Just hook yourself on behind Mr. Plow, and we'll be getting along."

The Harrow hooked himself on behind the Plow, and with much noise, Rattler started off again, followed by his friends.

"Well, well, where's this fine big parade going, I wonder?" some one said, just as they began to move along.

They stopped and looked around, and there they saw Mr. Wheat Drill, all bright with a shining new coat of paint. He was the fellow who sowed the little grains of wheat and covered them up in just the right way so that they would sprout and grow their very best.

"Why, if it isn't Mr. Wheat Drill!" cried Rattler. "Perhaps you would like to come along with us. We're all tired of standing still doing nothing this splendid holiday. We're going down to the big field to see where we shall all be working tomorrow."

"How interesting!" said the Wheat Drill. "I'm as full as I can be of wheat seed, all ready for tomorrow's work, and I shall enjoy seeing where I shall have to sow it."

"Well, just hook yourself on behind Mr. Harrow, then," said Rattler, "and we'll all be getting along to the big field."

"May I go, too?" rumbled the deep voice of the big fat Roller, who was standing beside his friend, the Wheat Drill.

"The more, the merrier!" laughed Rattler. "If you'll hook yourself on behind Mr. Drill, I can take you along nicely."

So the fat Roller hooked himself on behind the Drill, and Mr. Wheat Drill took his place behind the Harrow. Together they all clanked away, the big Tractor in the lead, with the Plow and the Harrow and the Wheat Drill and the Roller following along behind him. All were going to look at the big field where they had to start working the next day.

At last they came to the field. "It is a large field, isn't it?" remarked the Plow. "Mr. Rattler, you're going to be very tired before you finish pulling my shares through all this ground."

"You'll be more tired than ever before you drag us over it, to crush the clods and smooth the soil," said the Harrow and Roller.

"And you'll be most tired of all by the time you have pulled me around and I have sown wheat all over this big field," said the Drill.

"Tut-tut!" Rattler answered them. "All of you together couldn't make me really tired. Why, I can pull you while you work the big field, all at the same time, without its bothering me."

"Ha-ha-ha!" laughed the Plow, amused by such boasting.

"Ho-ho-ho!" laughed the others, also; for they thought Rattler was just trying to be funny.

"Of course I can," said the big Tractor again, just a little angry because they were laugh-

"I'm a very strong Tractor, I am."

"Ho-ho-ho-ho!" they all

ALL MORNING RATTLER PULLED HIS FRIENDS BACK AND FORTH

ing at him. "Shall I show you?"

"Do you mean to say," asked the astonished Plow, "that you can pull all of us, together, over this big field, while we do our work at the same time, without having to stop and rest?"

"Exactly," boasted Rattler.

laughed again. "You'll have to show us."

"I'll do just that very thing," cried Rattler, a little angrier than before. "Set your shares so they will bite deeply, Mr. Plow. And fix your teeth so that they will chew up all the big clods, Mr.

Harrow. And you, Mr. Drill, and you, Mr. Roller, just follow along and drop your seeds and smooth

back and forth across the field, followed by his friends. The Plow, just behind him, turned

—WHEN NOON CAME, HALF OF THE FIELD WAS DONE

out the soil again just as you always do."

The Plow set his shares so that they would bite deeply into the ground, and the others got all ready to do their work. Then the big Tractor, with his motor roaring loudly, began to clank

the fresh black soil in deep furrows, and the sharp teeth of the Harrow chewed up the big lumps so that the Wheat Drill behind him could drop his seeds and cover them. And the Roller made the ground smooth.

All morning Rattler pulled

his friends back and forth, back and forth, across the big field. When noon came, half of the field was done. But the big Tractor never stopped. All through the long afternoon he roared on, back and forth, back and forth—clank, clank! chuff, chuff! At last, by the time the sun was near setting, the whole big field had been plowed and harrowed and sown with wheat and rolled.

"What a very strong Tractor you are!" the Plow said to Rattler, when the Drill had planted his last grain of wheat. "I apologize for laughing at you, but I never thought any Tractor could be so strong." All the others joined Mr. Plow in telling Rattler what a really remarkable fellow he was.

The big Tractor was very pleased and happy, and though he was somewhat tired, he didn't

mind that at all. He thanked his friends for the pleasant things they said to him, and then he pulled them all back to their places in the barn lot. At last he clanked into his own shed, thinking what a wonderful day it had been.

That evening, when Mike, the Hired Man, came home from the Fair, he stopped in to see the big Tractor and make sure that he was ready for work the next day.

"Well, Rattler," said Mike, "and how did you enjoy your holiday?"

"Fine!" exclaimed Rattler. "It was the happiest day I have ever known!"

"What did you do with yourself all day?" Mike wanted to know.

The big Tractor began to tell the Hired Man just how he and his companions had spent their holiday. Mike was so surprised that he could say nothing at all, at first. Next, he began laughing so hard that he couldn't say anything then, either. And at last he rushed from the shed, still laughing so hard that the big tears rolled from his eyes.

As for Rattler, he never did learn what Mike found so funny in the way he had spent his wonderful holiday.

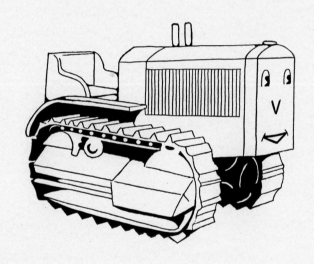

The Motor Boat That Went to School

"P UT, put, put, put!" said the new Motor Boat as he swung around toward the dock where all the other Boats were moored. "Well, well, how are you all?" he called to them, as his owner tied him up and sprang out on the pier. "My name is Arrow, and I'm called that because I can go so fast."

The other Boats just stared at him, hardly knowing what to say. He was very new and shiny, and most of them were old and dingy. They felt a little backward about becoming friendly too quickly with this newcomer.

"This seems to be a nice little lake," Arrow went on. "My master says that it is one of the nicest in this part of the country. Are there many Boats on it besides you at the dock here? Are there many fish in the lake? I hate to have messy fish caught and thrown about in me, don't you? Do they have any Motor Boat races here?"

And so the new Motor Boat went on and on, without giving

the other Boats a chance to answer any of his questions. They thought that he was a very strange Boat, because he talked so much. But they were already beginning to like him because he seemed friendly and very good natured to all.

After a few days, the other Boats began to feel that they knew Arrow a little better, and they began to answer some of his questions. Soon Arrow knew almost as much about the lake as they did.

He learned the names of all the Boats, and from the things they said he learned, also, what kind of people their masters were.

He found out who lived in all the houses that were built around that part of the lake. Before long he knew what all the buildings were in the little town that stood by the water's edge, near the dock where the Motor Boats were tied fast. There was one little white building in the town that interested him very much. It stood quite near the lake, and its smooth, green lawn ran right down to the water's edge.

"What is that pretty white building, with the big trees beside it and the green lawn that reaches down to the lake's shore?" he asked one day.

"Oh, that?" replied one of the Boats. "That is just the village school, where the children all go to learn to read and write, and to be educated in other things."

"How wonderful!" cried Arrow. "I wish I could go to school and be educated. Don't you? Of course, I already know a very great deal for a Motor Boat. I know that two added to two makes four; also, that two times two gives the same number. But what I can't figure out is why when three is added to three in the same way, it makes six, but three times three doesn't make six at all. Perhaps if I went to school I might learn why."

The other Motor Boats laughed.

"Schools are all right for human beings," said one of them, "but of what use is two times two to a Motor Boat? I prefer just to lie here in the water, or to make a trip over it once in a while, rather than to bother myself

"THAT IS THE VILLAGE SCHOOL, WHERE THE CHILDREN LEARN TO READ"

thinking about going to school and learning useless things."

"Oh, but going to school helps make you educated," said Arrow. "And when you are educated, you should be wise in many things. Now it seems to me that there are many times when a Motor Boat would be better off for having a little wisdom."

"Ho-hum! Perhaps so," said the big, slow Motor Boat that was tied up beside Arrow. "But why bother yourself about it? If wisdom is needed, let our masters supply it, say I."

"Yes," agreed Arrow, "perhaps you are right. But, still, it would be very nice if Motor Boats as well as children could go to school and learn things. I'm sure I should enjoy school very much."

And then, since all the other Boats at the dock laughed at him for having such funny ideas, Ar-

row said no more about the matter. But every time he looked across the water toward the little white schoolhouse, he wished that he might go there and learn things. And when he hurried past it, over the sparkling waters of the lake, and heard the school children playing in the yard at recess, he wanted to go to school more than ever.

Of course, it was rather foolish for a Motor Boat to think of going to school. Any other Boat except Arrow would soon have forgotten all about the matter. But he was quite a peculiar fellow, and he could not forget it.

"Perhaps some day I shall get the chance to go to school," he kept telling himself.

So the days went along, some of them bright and sunshiny and some of them dark and cloudy. And then, one evening, a big storm came up over the lake.

The wind blew so hard that it made the water of the lake roll up in big waves. The waves and the wind together tossed all the Boats about as they lay in the water tied to the dock. Where they had not been tied with great care, the storm made them bump hard against one another and against the dock.

Arrow bounded and bounced around on the water at a great rate. He was bumped so many times that some of his fresh, bright paint was rubbed off. But he did not mind, because he was having so much fun bouncing about on the storm waves. He kept jerking and tugging at the line that tied him fast to the dock, and all at once he jerked so hard that the line broke right in two.

"Look out, Arrow!" all the other Boats called to him as a big wave rolled him away from the dock. "Look out, or the storm will wreck you!"

Arrow could not answer them because the heavy waves were rolling him away toward the center of the lake. He was shaken up and down, and around and around, and he was rocked from side to side. Foam from the tops of the waves rolled into him. He was jerked and spun about so much that in a few minutes the poor Motor Boat didn't have the least idea where he was.

And then, a sudden flash of bright lightning showed him a little white building far away across the rolling, angry water.

"Why, that's the schoolhouse!" Arrow said to himself. "My goodness, but this storm has taken me a long way in a very short time. I must do something about it, right away, or else I shall never get back to the dock where I belong."

THE HEAVY WAVES WERE ROLLING ARROW TOWARD THE CENTER OF THE LAKE

So the Motor Boat waited until an extra big wave came rushing by, rolling with a great deal of foam on toward the shore where the white schoolhouse stood. He let himself be lifted and carried along by the great wave as it swiftly ran. The wind, blowing strongly against their backs, made them go faster than ever.

They rolled along so quickly that, before Arrow knew it, they were almost upon the shore. The big wave began to break up as it felt the sand of the shore coming up under it, and it curled over with a great hissing of froth and foam. The Motor Boat tried to stop himself in a great hurry, also, but he was going too fast. Almost before he knew what was happening the wave had thrown him right up on the schoolhouse lawn that grew down to the water's edge.

And there, because he was still going very fast and because the grass was so smooth, he just slid along on his keel, like a sled on runners, right toward the white schoolhouse. And because he was sliding fast and couldn't stop himself, he slid right on into the schoolhouse itself.

"Bang! Crash!" went the door as he hit it with his nose, and "Ouch!" cried Arrow. He felt his sides being pinched by the door frame as he slid through it. At last, inside the little white schoolhouse, he finally stopped and came to rest. His nose was pressed up against the teacher's desk, his sides were pushing the pupils' desks out of place, and his tail was sticking out through the door.

It was so very dark and everything had happened so quickly that the Motor Boat hadn't the least idea where he was. But he

$$416 \times 45 \qquad 719 \times 32 \qquad 361 \times 49 \qquad 428 \times 23 \qquad 61 \times 8$$

HIS NOSE WAS PRESSED UP AGAINST THE TEACHER'S DESK

was glad to have weathered the storm as well as he had, and it wasn't long until he fell fast asleep.

He woke up when the first light of morning began to come through the windows and looked around him to see where he was.

"Why, I must be in the schoolhouse!" he told himself, as he saw the blackboards and the desks and the books. "Just think of it, I've come to school at last!" And he kept on looking about him with very particular interest in everything he saw, because, being in school, he wanted to learn all he possibly could.

When the teacher and pupils came to school that morning, they were greatly surprised to find that a Motor Boat had been carried right into their schoolhouse by the storm. Soon nearly everybody in the little town was down in the school yard to see the strange sight. Many people took pictures of the Motor Boat that had gone to school. Arrow felt quite proud of himself when he saw how much attention he was attracting.

"My goodness, but everybody is excited about my being here!" he said to himself. "I'm

MANY PEOPLE TOOK PICTURES OF THE MOTOR BOAT THAT HAD GONE TO SCHOOL

sure I must be the very first Motor Boat that ever went to school. My friends at the dock can't laugh at me any more when I talk about going there."

Before long, a great many men began working hard to get the Motor Boat out of the schoolhouse and back on the water of the lake where he belonged. They finally pulled him out of the building, put rollers under his keel, and rolled him down into the water. Then they patched the leaks which the storm had made in him and ran him back to his place at the dock. There they tied him again with

—ARROW FELT QUITE PROUD OF THE ATTENTION HE WAS ATTRACTING

a strong rope that he could not break.

Poor Arrow's paint was all scratched and scraped away, and his nose was rather dented from hitting the schoolhouse door so hard. There were other parts about him that no longer looked as fine as they used to look. But Arrow did not seem to mind these things in the least, and the other Boats didn't, either.

Instead, all of his friends at the dock were so interested in hearing Arrow's story of how he had gone to school that they could talk of nothing else. They never laughed at him again, and because they always remembered that he had gone to school, they were certain he must surely be the wisest Motor Boat in the whole world — as perhaps, indeed, he was.

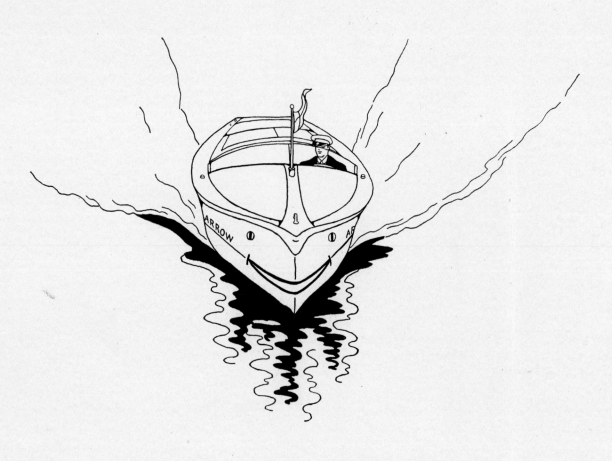